MULBERRY BOOKS · New York

Copyright © 1988 by John Steptoe. All rights reserved. No part
of this book may be reproduced or utilized in any form or by any means,
electronic or mechanical, including photocopying, recording or by any
information storage and retrieval system, without permission in writing
from the Publisher. Inquiries should be addressed to Lothrop, Lee
& Shepard Books, a division of William Morrow & Company, Inc.,
1350 Avenue of the Americas, New York, NY 10019.
Printed in Singapore.
First Mulberry Edition, 1992.   10 9 8 7 6 5 4 3 2 1

Library of Congress Cataloging in Publication Data
Steptoe, John, 1950-1989. Baby says.
Summary: A baby and big brother figure out how to get along.
[1. Brothers—Fiction. 2. Babies—Fiction.
3. Afro-Americans—Fiction.] I. Title. PZ7.S8367Bab
1992   [E]—dc20   92-11524   ISBN 0-688-11855-0

Baby Says

John Steptoe

"Uh, oh."

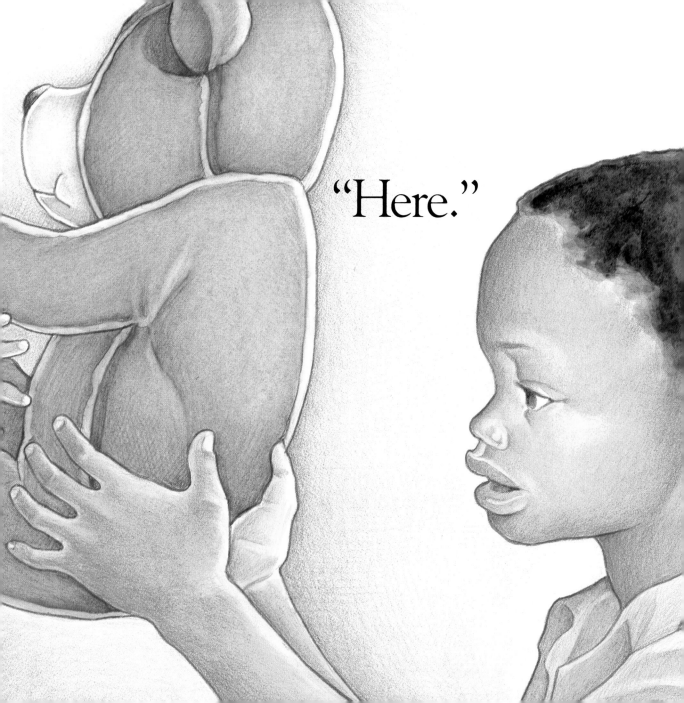

"Here."

"Uh, oh."

"No, no."

"No, no!"

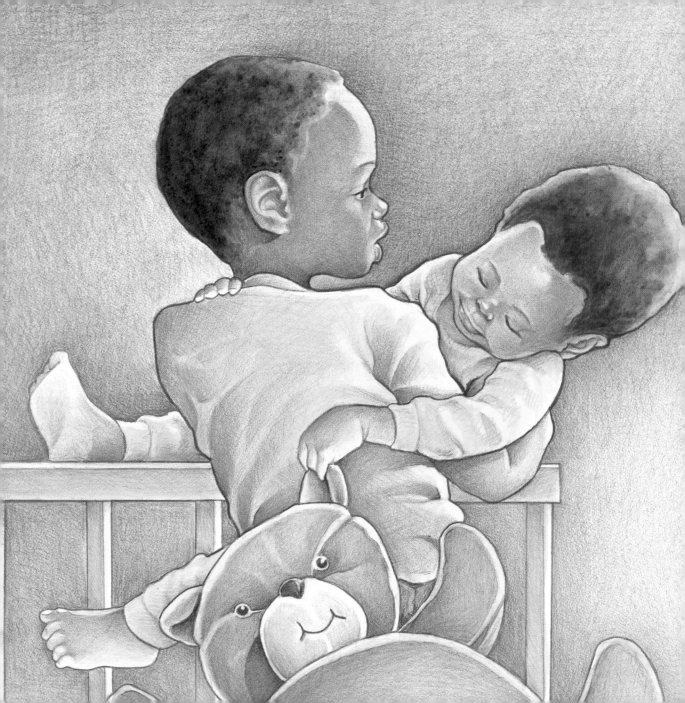

"Okay, okay."

"Okay.
Uh, oh.
No, no."

"Uh, oh.
No, no."

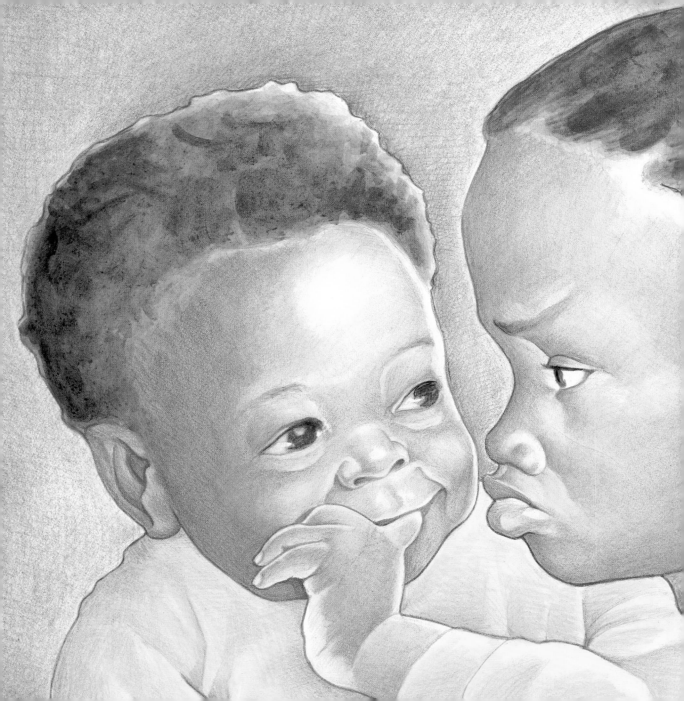

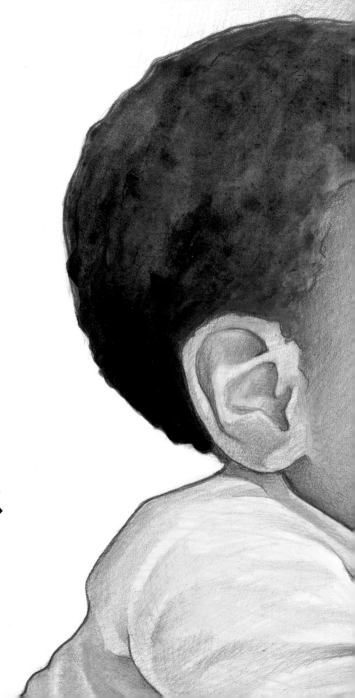

"Okay, baby.
Okay."

Baby says,
"Okay!"